Zach Apologizes

William Mulcahy

illustrated by
Darren McKee

free spirit
PUBLISHING®

Library of Congress Cataloging-in-Publication Data
Mulcahy, William.
  Zach apologizes / William Mulcahy ; illustrated by Darren McKee.
    p. cm. — (Zach rules series)
  ISBN 978-1-57542-389-0
  1. Apologizing—Juvenile literature. I. McKee, Darren. II. Title.
  BF575.A75M85 2012
  395.1'22—dc23
                                                                                          2011032895

eBook ISBN: 978-1-57542-670-9

Reading Level Grades 2 & 3; Interest Level Ages 5–8;
Fountas & Pinnell Guided Reading Level M

Edited by Eric Braun
Cover and interior design by Tasha Kenyon

10 9 8 7 6 5 4 3 2 1
Printed in the United States of America
B10950212

Free Spirit Publishing Inc.
Minneapolis, MN
(612) 338-2068
help4kids@freespirit.com
www.freespirit.com

Free Spirit offers competitive pricing.
Contact edsales@freespirit.com for pricing information on multiple quantity purchases.

Dedication

To Jane for always believing

Acknowledgments

Thanks to those who have supported my writing and counseling journey.

In the early days: Donna, Mike, Bobby T., Mac, John, Maura, Kevin, Banks, and Mellon

In the middle days: Larry, Nan and Suzie, Len, Sister Sheila, Helene, Andrea, Deb Vest, and Prosser

These days: Brenda, Sonya, Ben, Laura Cherone, Laura Pals, Kristin, and the Neasers

Throughout: my family

Special thanks to Dr. Bob Schedgick for suggesting the apology model. Lastly, to John Kober and Eric Braun and all the folks at Free Spirit: Thanks for taking a chance.

Alex was playing with Zach's robo-rocket cruiser . . . again.

It made Zach so mad he forgot all about his manners and pushed his little brother down.

1

That's when Mom interrupted. "Enough!" she said.

"Zach, give me the spaceship and go cool down."

Zach went to his room.

He knew he'd hurt his brother, but he didn't want to think about it.

5

After a while, Zach gave up.
He felt too scrambled up inside to do anything.
Then he heard a knock at the door.

"How are you feeling?" Mom asked.
She could tell he was upset about
what happened.

"Crummy."

"I think I can help," Mom said.
"I want to show you how to apologize."

"Apologize? Do I have to?"

"It always makes **me** feel better," she said.

"Besides, I know you can handle this. It's called the four-square apology."

Mom handed Zach a pencil. She showed him how to do the four-square apology. "You have to think really hard about what happened, and then fill in each of these squares," she explained. "You can write or draw. In the first square, write or draw what you did to hurt Alex."

Zach thought about what happened.
What did he do to hurt Alex?
He wrote, "Pushed Alex down."

1. What I did to hurt someone

2. How the

PUSheD
Alex down

...do next time

4

9

Mom said, "In the next square, you have to say how you think it made him feel."

This was hard. Until now, Zach had only thought about how he felt. How would it feel to be shoved by your brother?

Finally he remembered the look on Alex's face. Zach had made him cry.

"Sad and hurt," he wrote in the square.

...at I did to hurt someone

PUSheD Alex down

2. How the person felt!

sad AND hurt

Mom pointed to square number three. "What could you do next time instead of pushing? After you think of a good idea, draw or write it in this square."

Zach thought of some ideas.

Just grab my toy and run.

Take something of his and promise to break it unless he gives back my robo-rocket cruiser.

3. What I can do next time

4. Hou

ASK fOR
The tOy

But those were just pretend ideas. Zach knew a better answer.

"That's easy!" he said. "Ask for the toy." His dad always reminded him to use his words. Sometimes it was hard to remember when he was mad, though.

"One left," Mom said. "The last square is about how you can make it up to him."

"Make it up?" Zach asked.

"Pushing him down hurt him—that was wrong," she said. "What can you do to make things right again?"

"I don't know," Zach said. What did she mean? He couldn't go back in a time machine and change what he did.

"Maybe you could do something special for him," Mom suggested. "Like do his chore for the week."

Zach already had chores. He didn't want to feed the dog, too. He got an idea. He wrote, "Do you want to play with the robo-rocket cruiser?"

Mom looked over Zach's four-square apology. "I think Alex will appreciate this," she said. "When you're ready, put your apology into action. You can take the sheet with you.

"And remember, Zach: You're a good person even though you did something wrong."

Zach went over his four squares again. He decided he was ready.

Zach felt his heart bumping in his chest. This was not going to be easy. What if Alex laughed at him? What if Zach's apology didn't make either of them feel better?

He gripped the paper tightly and remembered what his mom said about being a good person even if you do something wrong. He was glad she said that.

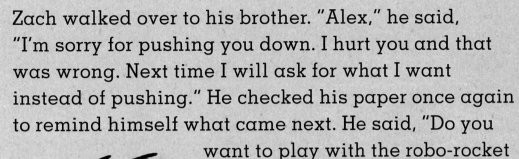

Zach walked over to his brother. "Alex," he said, "I'm sorry for pushing you down. I hurt you and that was wrong. Next time I will ask for what I want instead of pushing." He checked his paper once again to remind himself what came next. He said, "Do you want to play with the robo-rocket cruiser and some of my other ships?"

Alex thought for a second. "Can we play together?"

Zach's heart relaxed. "Does that mean you accept my apology?"

His brother nodded and hugged him.

"Then let's go outside!" Zach said.

"Can I be the alien?" Alex asked.

"Sure!"

When Zach apologizes, he tries as hard as he can to fix the hurt he caused. He helps his brother feel better, and when that happens, Zach feels better, too.

1. What I did to hurt somebody

2. How the person felt

3. What I can do next time

4. How I'll make it up to the person

Apologizing can be hard! If you need help apologizing, you can use Zach's four-square apology. Make a square on a piece of paper. Draw lines to divide it into four smaller squares. Fill in the squares with your answers to the steps above. You can use words or pictures. When you're done, put your apology into action. If you've done something wrong or hurtful, you can make it right again, just like Zach did. Apologizing takes courage, but you can do it!

Helping Children Apologize

Apologizing can be hard to do, especially for young children. It means admitting they have done something wrong and asking for forgiveness. Children often feel an avalanche of thoughts and feelings when they have hurt someone, and apologizing can feel shameful if not taught in a positive way. This is especially true when adults force children to say they're sorry. A forced apology is often meaningless and even traumatic. It can compromise relationships and an individual's well-being.

But apologizing can and should be a positive, healthy act for both the giver and receiver. A sincere apology keeps everyone's dignity intact and repairs the wrong that has been done. Such an apology has the power to

- end conflict without fighting
- encourage further communication
- restore self-respect
- improve empathy for both the giver and receiver
- repair damaged relationships
- heal negative feelings such as guilt, shame, and anger

The four-square apology presented in this book has four key parts. To make it positive and effective, you will want to partner with children in the apology process. Here are the four parts along with some tips to help you guide your child:

1. **What I did to hurt somebody.** Perhaps the hardest part of apologizing is admitting that, yes, I have done something wrong. I hurt someone—perhaps physically, perhaps emotionally. Allow children sufficient time to calm down and acknowledge what they've done. Know your child. Some children need ten minutes to settle themselves, while some need an hour. However, don't let too much time pass, or the apology will lose some of its meaning. When children are ready to talk about it, remind them that *everyone* makes mistakes, and everyone does something to hurt others sometimes. That does not mean the child is a bad person, just that he or she did a bad thing.

2. **How the person felt.** This step helps the apologizing child understand the impact of what he or she did. Empathy—to be aware of and understand the thoughts and feelings of others—is a critical social-emotional skill. It is key to developing a secure sense of self and healthy relationships. If children have difficulty with this step, ask them to picture themselves as the victim—to put themselves in the other person's shoes. How would *they* feel? Or has anyone ever hurt them in a similar way? How did that feel?

3. **What I can do next time.** This step helps children think about and plan for their future behavior, including promising to try not to be hurtful again. How will I handle similar situations? What are my options? What will I choose to do? Spend time helping your children discover the many choices they have in a given situation; choose an option based on what they value, not on a knee-jerk reaction. This will make it easier for them to keep their promises.

4. **How I'll make it up to the person.** This is often the crucial feature of an apology. When we hurt other people, we take away something from them. Only by giving something back can we truly repair this hurt. Suggest to children that the way they make it up to the other person might have something to do with the hurt they caused. In Zach's story, he pushed his brother over a toy. To make it up, he offers the toy and more. Children don't need to go overboard with what they offer. Their offer needs to be sincere and, of course, reasonably possible.

After children have answered all four parts of the four-square apology, they include the answers from *all four parts* when they deliver the apology. These answers are not only important for the apologizing child to think about, they also need to be heard by the person being apologized to. Kids don't have to recite their answers from the sheet word for word, but they can use them as a guide.

A few other tips:

- Perhaps the most important thing adults can do is model genuine apologies themselves. This gives children a strong message that apologizing is important. They see adults taking responsibility for their actions, and this helps reinforce that apologizing is not a sign of weakness but a sign of strength. It shows that the adult is honest, generous, and committed to improving relationships.

- Guide children *gently* to apologize—don't force an apology. Teach them the four-square apology well before it's needed, at a time when feelings are not running high, so children know what to expect. They also will know that you believe they can handle the responsibility. Talk about the good things apologizing can do, so when the time comes that an apology is needed, it won't feel like a punishment.

- Help children be as specific as possible about their answers for each of the four squares. If a child's answers seem vague, it might be because he or she doesn't fully understand the four-square apology, is having trouble taking responsibility for his or her actions, or is struggling to process what happened. Don't be afraid to use examples from your own life to walk the child through the apology, perhaps even verbalizing the internal dialogue you go through when preparing to apologize.

- Once a child apologizes, let that be the end of the episode. Don't hold a wrongdoing over the child's head. An apology is a way of turning a wrong into a right, to help everyone heal and learn from behavior. These messages are confused if the parent keeps reminding the child what he or she did or imposes some form of punishment. The act of apologizing is the "teachable moment."

- Let children know that not everyone will accept their apology. Some hurts take more time to heal than others. Regardless, guide children to do their part, in a sincere and honest way, to the best of their abilities. A sincere apology comes from our willingness to make amends and offer remorse—and not from what the other person will do. In addition to healing relationships, apologizing is essential to taking care of ourselves.

Teaching children to apologize authentically is one of the greatest gifts you can give. It helps them develop empathy, improve relationship skills, and learn responsibility for their actions. Healthy apologies today lead to healthier relationships tomorrow.

Download a printable copy of the four-square apology at www.freespirit.com/Apology.

About the Author

William Mulcahy is a licensed professional counselor, psychotherapist, and supervisor of the Cooperative Parenting Center at Family Service of Waukesha, Wisconsin. He has served as a consultant at Stillwaters Cancer Support Center in Wisconsin, specializing in grief and cancer-related issues, and he has worked with children with special needs. Bill's short stories have appeared in several publications. The Zach Rules books are his first books for children, merging his passions for good storytelling and providing counseling-like tools to help children live healthier, happier lives. Bill lives in Summit, Wisconsin, with his three sons, who played their own role in the creation of the Zach Rules series. His website is wmulcahy.com.

About the Illustrator

Darren McKee has illustrated books for many publishers over his 20-year career. When not working, he spends his time riding his bike, reading, drawing, and traveling. He lives in Dallas, Texas, with his wife Debbie.

More Great Books from Free Spirit

Zach Gets Frustrated
by William Mulcahy, illustrated by Darren McKee

Zach and his family go to the beach, but Zach is having a lousy day. He dropped his toothbrush in the toilet, his best friend went to someone else's birthday party instead of joining him, and most frustrating of all, he can't get his kite to fly! Zach kicks sand, yells angry words, and asks his dad if they can just go home now. Instead, his dad teaches him a simple, three-step approach to get a handle on frustration and find a way to enjoy himself even when things aren't going his way. The three-point strategy is presented as the three corners of a triangle and is illustrated using the corners of Zach's kite. Kids will easily understand and remember this tool. *32 pp., illust., 4-color, H/C, 8" x 8". Ages 5–8.*

Our Emotions and Behavior Series
by Sue Graves, illustrated by Desideria Guicciardini

Small children have big feelings. The Our Emotions and Behavior series uses cheerful, brightly illustrated stories to help kids understand how their emotions and actions are related—and how they can learn to manage both. Follow along as Noah, Ben, Nora, and their friends discover ways to deal with fears, sadness, rules, and sharing. At the end of each book, a two-page series of pictures invites kids to tell a story in their own words. A special section for adults suggests discussion questions and ideas for guiding children to talk about their feelings. *Each book: 32 pp., illust., 4-color, H/C, 7¾" x 9½". Ages 4–8.*

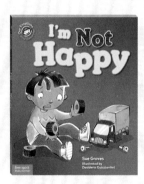   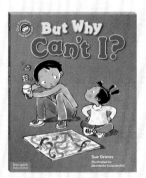

Interested in purchasing multiple quantities? Contact edsales@freespirit.com or call 1.800.735.7323 and ask for Education Sales.

Many Free Spirit authors are available for speaking engagements, workshops, and keynotes. Contact speakers@freespirit.com or call 1.800.735.7323.

For pricing information, to place an order, or to request a free catalog, contact:

free spirit PUBLISHING®

217 Fifth Avenue North • Suite 200 • Minneapolis, MN 55401-1299
toll-free 800.735.7323 • local 612.338.2068 • fax 612.337.5050
help4kids@freespirit.com • www.freespirit.com